PRESENTED TO:

_____

FROM:

_____

DATE:

_____

THE COW SAID NEIGH!

A FARM STORY

BY RORY FEEK

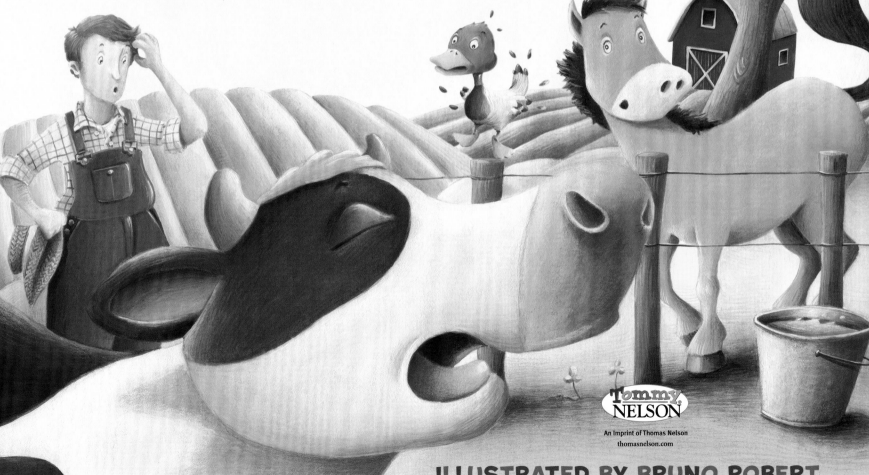

Tommy NELSON®

An Imprint of Thomas Nelson
thomasnelson.com

ILLUSTRATED BY BRUNO ROBERT

Published in Nashville, Tennessee, by Tommy Nelson. Tommy Nelson is an imprint of Thomas Nelson. Thomas Nelson is a registered trademark of HarperCollins Christian Publishing, Inc.

Published in association with Atticus Brand Partners, 611 Shenandoah Drive, Brentwood, Tennessee 37027.

Tommy Nelson titles may be purchased in bulk for educational, business, fund-raising, or sales promotional use. For information, please e-mail SpecialMarkets@ ThomasNelson.com.

Any Internet addresses, phone numbers, or company or product information printed in this book are offered as a resource and are not intended in any way to be or to imply an endorsement by Thomas Nelson, nor does Thomas Nelson vouch for the existence, content, or services of these sites, phone numbers, companies, or products beyond the life of this book.

Library of Congress Cataloging-in-Publication Data is on file.
ISBN 978-1-4003-1171-2

Printed in China

18 19 20 21 22 DSC 10 9 8 7 6 5 4 3 2 1

Mfr: DSC / Shenzhen, China / September 2018 / PO #9492428

to Indiana

There once was a cow in a barn who could see
A horse in a field who ran wild and free.
"If I were a horse, I could run free all day."
And the cow opened his mouth and let out a big . . .

The horse heard the cow, and he looked in the pond
At the duck with the bill who swam all day long.
"If I were a duck, bet they'd stay off my back."
And the horse reared back, and out came a . . .

The duck heard the horse, and he saw the sheep
With a big winter coat, two inches deep.
"If I were a sheep, that would be good."
And the duck said . . .

BAA!

. . . as loud as he could.

The sheep heard the duck, and he looked at the pig
Using his nose in the deep mud to dig.
"If I were a pig, I could dig with my snout."
And the sheep opened his mouth, and an . . .

OINK! . . . came out.

The pig heard the sheep, and he looked in the yard
At the dog on the porch who proudly stood guard.
"If I were a dog, I bet I could be tough."
And the pig wiggled his tail, and he let out a . . .

RUFF!

The dog heard the pig, and he looked in the house
At the cat on the rug that was chasing a mouse.
"If I were a cat, I'd be inside right now."
And the dog opened his mouth and let out a . . .

The cat heard the dog, and he left the mouse there
And looked at the farmer asleep in his chair.
"If I were a man, oh, the places I'd go."
And then the cat purred and let out a . . .

HELLO!

The farmer opened his eyes when he heard the cat,

And he thought to himself, *Did I really hear that?*

Then he walked to the barn, and he opened the door
And heard some more things he'd not heard before.

The cow said

NEIGH,

and
the horse
said

QUACK.

The duck said **BAA,**

and the sheep **OINKED** back.

The pig said

RUFF,

and the dog said

MEOW,

As the cat and the farmer stood by the cow.

Then the farmer smiled.
What else could he do
But open his mouth and let out a big . . .

MOOOOOO!